# The Opposite of
# Swedish Death Cleaning

*For my Mum & Dad*
*for gifting me the opposite of Swedish death cleaning*

*And for Emily*
*who is alongside me in it all*

# The Opposite of
# Swedish Death Cleaning

*Alison Binney*

**SEREN**

Seren is the book imprint of
Poetry Wales Press Ltd.
Suite 6, 4 Derwen Road, Bridgend,
Wales, CF31 1LH

www.serenbooks.com
Follow us on social media @SerenBooks

The right of Alison Binney to be identified as
the author of this work has been asserted in accordance
with the Copyright, Designs and Patents Act, 1988.

ISBN: 978-1-78172-775-1
ebook: 978-1-78172-776-8

A CIP record for this title is available from the British Library.

The publisher acknowledges the financial assistance of the Books Council of Wales.

EU GPSR Authorised Representative
Logos Europe, 9 rue Nicolas Poussin, 17000,
La Rochelle, France
E-mail: Contact@logoseurope.eu

Cover artwork: Kate Winter
Author photograph: Emily McMullen

Printed in Bembo by 4Edge ltd, Hockley.

# Contents

Inside the house of delirium                                          7
Muscle memory                                                         8
27 reasons why we don't play the furniture game when I visit          9
The opposite of Swedish death cleaning                               10
Orange or lemon?                                                     11
The philosopher's axe                                                12
The way you knew                                                     13
The L word                                                           14
Sestina for a lost boi                                               15
Sunday School                                                        17
Testimony                                                            18
Party Susan                                                          19
The mysterious starling                                              20
The lost words                                                       21
How to conquer nature                                                22
38.7°                                                                23
Skyler and Jeff move in                                              24
Late                                                                 25
Everyday heterosexual predicaments: the soap opera                   26
Colin arrives in Albert Square                                       27
Haircut, 17                                                          28
Night run                                                            29
The hard miles                                                       30
Middle-aged       alone       no dog                                 31
Missing woman joins search party looking for herself                 32
Basic life support class                                             34
Pomander                                                             35
Dark Peak, February                                                  36
Pandemic recovery plan                                               37
What they didn't teach us on the PGCE                                38
Chalk                                                                39
Weight                                                               40
Spice rack                                                           42
Come to the cookhouse door                                           43
When you give a plant to a teacher                                   44
Ditton Meadow                                                        46
Desire lines                                                         48
Straight-line mission                                                49
On stagnant deeps                                                    50
Heeling in at Lower Wood                                             51

On Wonder Woman's Island     52
Courtship     53
How we knew     54
Opening     55
Exposure     56
When we hold hands     57
Like a fish     58
Everyday heterosexual predicaments: the mini break     59
Tea & coffee at 8.25     60
Sleeping together     61
Grain     62
Pitch drop experiment     63
Christmas Eve in Dad's kitchen     64
Distance     65
Guinea pig     66
I cut, you choose     67
Sunday lunch     68
The women of 10y3     69
The speed of spring     70
Quinquireme     71
Shed     72

Notes     73
Acknowledgements     75

# Inside the house of delirium

The curtains sleep until midday.
The smoke alarm coughs behind its hand.
The mirror is nervous of strangers.
The sock in the bath has forgotten its partner's name.
The razor is full of spiders.
The milk doesn't want to be a burden.
The biscuits think it's June 2015.
The mug recites the sea areas and coastal weather stations.
The pendulum has lost the word *tock*.
The radio knows who the Prime Minister is but won't say.
The remote is late for work and has run out of pants.
The teapot can't remember if it takes sugar.
The washing machine rocks in the corner.
The fridge hums an old hymn.
The cooker hunts for its keys.
The microwave counts backwards from one hundred in sevens, gets stuck on 88.
The light bulb prefers the dark.
The computer frets about terminal illness.
The lawn hasn't shaved for weeks.
The newspapers are ganging up.
The bed dreams about locked toilets
and wakes too late.

# Muscle memory

Three weeks earlier I'd said *My Dad has Alzheimer's*
to the sashed woman in the porch who swept me
past the kiosk through the transept to the vestry.
The first time I'd said it aloud: I sounded older,
as if I knew just what you needed and how to find it.
She offered me up to the vergers – *This lady is enquiring
about Christmas Eve. Her father has Alzheimer's* –
who tumbled over themselves to show how welcome you'd be,
dementia and all, while I stood like a lost child in a shop.

So, at the end of the year of lost things, we came here,
to sit by the copper font that stretched our faces like toffee,
where giant candelabra breathed wax down the nave,
and the cathedral cat slipped between chairs and feet
to bag a warm vent. And where, when the organ rumbled
the chords of *Hark the Herald*, you pushed yourself up
on the frame to stand straight-backed, singing the bass line
by heart while the great west door swung open.

# 27 reasons why we don't play the furniture game when I visit

*after Simon Armitage*

Your roof is an upside-down shoe on a park railing
and your driveway is an eggshell of cress
and your doorstep is a loose tooth
and your windows are a fungal toenail infection.
Your birdbath is a mug left on the staffroom windowsill.
And your books are inaudible announcements on the last train home
and your filing cabinet is a shark hosting a parasitic worm
and your houseplants are unposted thank-you letters
and your clock is a coastguard hut at night.
Your curtains are size 22 dresses on the end of a sales rail
and your mattress is the surface of a bar during lockdown
and the whole system of your electrics is our turn with the class guinea pig.
Your carpet is a warm glass of wine in the interval of a church concert
and your calendar is an unclaimed raffle prize.
And your fridge is a squashed can on a Sunday morning
and your pantry is an abandoned wormery
and your cutlery drawer is the bottom of a crisp packet
and your toilet is a condemned colliery.
Your striplight is the smile of a missing child
and your radio is a catfight in the small hours
and your dining table is the second-placed conker in a playground tournament
and your back door is a double decker bus stuck under the railway bridge
and your front door is a blown fairy light.
And your armchair is a muntjac deer on the hard shoulder
and your coathook is a hard shoulder.
Your photos are an explosion of pigeon feathers on the lawn.

When you ask me, my words are a string of silk handkerchiefs.

# The opposite of Swedish death cleaning

Lately, I conjure a woman in Stockholm
opening her father's front door into laminate light,
the scent of lemons. Crossing the hall to his study,
she finds the folder marked *Död* in an otherwise
empty desk, and heads for the kitchen – one chair,
one mug, one teaspoon, one coffee filter left.

I want an antonym for *döstädning*, these days,
for we are not Swedish, and this is messy,
you in the home, not yet dead, me frisking
your house for Ladybird books and egg cups,
stamp albums, paperweights and pebbles,
for fifty nubs of Imperial Leather soap.

My Swedish double rinses her father's mug,
leaves it to drain while she makes a few calls,
then slips it into her bag. Perhaps it will hold
her toothbrush. Perhaps, on the train home,
a line from a bedtime poem will hum
for a moment, then mumble itself to sleep.

# Orange or lemon?

I scroll through photos of caterpillars
on the ragwort they've ravaged this week.

You recall masters, stump-legged from the war,
armed with lamps and cyanide jars.

In the latest shot, six cinnabars hug six stalks.
We ponder the end game,

whether I'll wake to one huge moth,
ravenous, thumping the patio door.

A carer comes in, a jug in each hand,
offering orange or lemon.

You like both, so it shouldn't matter,
except on the train home, I'll think how long

you chewed that question over,
the carer standing with the two jugs,

me saying *you had lemon last time,
why not mix it up?* you saying *well now,*

*there's a question*, the caterpillars
keeping shtum, the moth beating.

# The philosopher's axe

In a pub somewhere, someone is telling
somebody else they're literally not the same

person they were seven years ago, citing
that thing about cells regenerating every few

years, while, in another pub, somebody claims
that's a myth based on the average of, say,

the five-day lives of intestinal epithelial cells,
the growth of toenails by one millimetre per month,

the replacement of hippocampal neurons
every twenty to thirty years. But your Achilles

knows you are no Ship of Theseus, no
philosophical conundrum. Ask the scar

at the base of your thumb if it's still
the same axe. Ask the nick in your heart.

# The way you knew

the way you knew your own coat in the cloakroom    the way you knew
as you chewed how big the next bubble would be    the way everyone
knew the new boy was weird even before he began drinking ink    the
way you knew how to share crisps and when to and why it mattered    the
way your bike always knew the way home    the way you knew when to
laugh and how much and who with    the way you knew not to sit at the
front    the way you knew when to put your hand up and why no one
did any more    the way you knew not to wear shoes like that    the way
you knew what *behind the bike sheds* meant before anyone said    the way
everyone knew who went    the way you knew the name carved on the
desk wasn't yours but the *izza lezza* made you go red    the way you
knew not to wear your hair short    the way you knew how to walk
how to talk how to french kiss a boy and why you had to and more    the
way you knew for sure that if anyone knew about you you were dead

# The L Word

*Ms Healey's a lesbian.* He licked the first syllable
off the back of his front teeth like a bogey,
blew the b in our faces, spat the rest on the floor.

All that week the new word tainted our tongues
with the cling of a stamp. At home I turned it over
in my mouth, wondering what it meant

for funny, sparky Ms Healey with her glasses
and hair like mine. What did it mean for Martina
when Mum's lips pinched at the word?

In the garden, my brother was McEnroe;
I was Virginia Wade. Later it flicked like a spitball
from the back of the class, slid down the nape of my neck.

If you wiped it away, they knew it had stuck.
I kept it under my tongue like a piece of old gum
brought out to chew in the dark. When its bubble burst

on my lips I gulped it down. It's a lump in my gut
even now, something I swallowed whole and cannot bring up.
I can't take the taste away, so I settle for gay.

# Sestina for a lost boi

that day playing football with the boys
when the teacher told you
to put your top on you went home
knowing something had changed for good
no one said but you saw enough
to tell you didn't fit

any more on the pitch couldn't fit
even more with the girls eyeing the boys
whatever you were it was not enough
any which way you tried so you
tried instead to be good
and you got very good bringing home

top marks tucking into homework
sheets and textbooks fitting
in violin and guides and hockey so good
there was no time for boys
so they left you alone if you
could only fold small enough

no one would know there was enough
going on already and at home
it all depended on you
soon you found you could fit
in a corner of a pocket of the boys'
shorts you wore under your good

sunday dress it felt good
holding yourself in your palm enough
to know you were still there this not-boy
starting to find a home
inside the girl who'd never fit
in playground or church this you

15

you knew by touch this you
you couldn't yet name good
god but she was a perfect fit
and in time you had enough
of not feeling at home
and the endless talk of boys

took yourself out to find the clothes that fit
and one day sure enough you were finally good
to bring this beautiful boi home

# Sunday School

It takes ten years to advance along the corridor
from Beginners through Primary then Seniors,
before you're allowed upstairs
to play pool in the Soft Drinks Bar.
Now, you're in the Senior Room

with the Daycare Centre chairs that fart,
making matchbox books of the Bible
to display on the shelf below Jesus.
You're writing *Leviticus* in bubble letters
of gradually decreasing size.

You wish you'd got *Ruth*. Mrs Morris fires
revision questions for the Scripture Exam,
and you're thinking *Shadrach, Meshach and Abednego,
A golden calf, Galilee,* but you keep shtum.
You've all agreed Mrs Morris is wet.

There's 10p for the collection in your shoe.
Your brother spent his on a *Sunday Sport*
he's hidden under his shirt. You won't tell.
Probably. If he cleans the guinea pigs out.
It's your turn to put the biscuits on plates.

You flip the chocolate hobnobs upside down
so the adults won't take them first.
Mrs Morris launches into *I will make you
fishers of men* and you nudge your best friend
and sing *vicious old men* at the exact same time,

feeling the throb of her ribs against yours,
your laughs erupting in snorts,
smothered by broken chords.
Later, during coffee, you sneak back
to Beginners to sit in the tiny seats.

On the wall, the Cradle Roll, her name
just above yours. She licks all the chocolate
off her biscuit and tips back in her chair.
*What now?* she asks. And you both know what,
and that you can't. Not yet, not here. Someday. Maybe.

# Testimony

you have a hole in your
soul your breasts belong to
your future husband we
had a board meeting and
decided that you can no
longer serve you're not as
well-dressed as I thought
you would be that lifestyle
makes me want to take a
shower your life is an
abomination    I love you
very much I've stopped shopping at that supermarket that shows two men
cooking lasagne together in their home because I think they're normalising
something   disgusting we don't wave flags and hold street parades for proud
burglars maybe if you dressed more feminine and wore lipstick the way you use
love is far from the Christian way you have the theology of a five year old gay
people are the devil's droppings we'd like you to step down from children's
work it might be allowed but it's not God's best life for you my son is a police-
man and those gays are always trying to tell him they're victims and he says it's
so annoying is it possible
you were dropped on your
head at birth Jesus did not
accept everyone when you
celebrate holy communion
it turns into the body and
blood of the devil I have
a    duty  of  careto   the
congregation you're only
half a person the way you
live is abhorrent to God
but      you're      always
welcome if you follow
this path you will live a
very lonely life we love
you and are happy for you
to continue coming  to
church but we don't think it
appropriate  for  you  to
speak   can I pray for you?

# Party Susan

Mum brought it back, triumphant, from a Tupperware party,
a prize for the most accurate sketch of a husband, blindfold,
which she would never have won sighted,
but she had a secret knack for blindfold drawing:
she'd plant her other hand in the middle of the page
so her drawing hand always knew where it was.

My drawing hand would always know where it was,
I decided, should I be called upon to sketch the husband
for whom I would grate carrot, slice cucumber, cut cress,
rinse radishes, hard-boil eggs, carve tomatoes into roses,
and, having filled the Party Susan segments, snip chives
into the centre circle. I think I could draw him still,
blindfold, sitting at the kitchen table, helping himself
to a bit of everything, asking how the children got on at school.

# The mysterious starling

or 'Mauke starling' reads seven different languages,
is fluent in three. A lifelong vegetarian, she admits

*The species is known from a single skin. Its overall*
*length is 7.5 inches (19 cm). Bill from gape 1 inch*

her activist days are now behind her. In a recent questionnaire
she emerged as 'Mostly ds: Flamboyant completer-finisher'

*from anterior margin of nostril 1.25cm. Wing and tarsus*
*measurement are somewhat less than in the living bird*

although she is unsure how much credence to give this.
Her favourite colour is turquoise. If pressed, she describes herself

*due to shrinkage of the specimen. The other measurements*
*are from the freshly killed bird. Dull dusky black overall*

as a 'spiritual atheist'. She can cure others' hiccoughs, but not
her own. Her memory of the chemical elements remains undimmed

*with lighter brown feather edges which are prominent on the*
*body feathers and less conspicuous on the remiges*

which pleases her. She prefers not to discuss politics.
On holiday, she once tried marijuana. She has no truck

*and tail. Iris yellow. Feet dusky brownish; bill*
*the same colour or somewhat lighter.*

with conspiracy theorists. Yoga bores her. She adores hopping.
has been known to gallop on special birthdays, and famously

*The binomen Aplonis mavornata is the result of Buller's*
*misreading of the name inornarta on the specimen label.*

*As he genuinely believed this spelling to be correct,*
*the binomial, although it has no meaning, is valid.*

# The lost words

Nobody noticed at first:
while we scrolled
and skyped and tweeted,

they flapped and flitted
and beetled and slithered
and skittered and scurried

away. Later, we'd gape
at a big grey bird, probing
the gap in our minds

like a missing tooth.
*Let's look it up*, we'd say,
looking down at our little screens,

while the big grey bird
beat easy wings
into the golden clouds.

# How to conquer nature

*Mao Zedong: The 'Four Pests' campaign, 1958*

Know the sparrow is your enemy:
you cannot prosper with his beak in your grain.

Rise up, raid nests, gather pots and pans,
ladles and spoons, clatter the branches bare.

Take aim with rifle and slingshot.
Drum at the rooftops, until the weary

fall from the sky like rotten leaves.
Consider, as you leap forward,

if you'd rather eat parent or child.
Stop your ears to the song of locusts.

# 38.7°

*29th July 2019*

Good morning! And it is a glorious morning,
with a ridge of high pressure set fair over
the whole of the UK for the foreseeable future,
bringing plenty of sunshine and even the chance
of record-breaking temperatures later on.
Further afield, in the far east, low-lying land
will give way to rising sea levels, with just
a possibility of one or two nations vanishing
before noon. To the south, a band of famine
will creep further inland throughout the day,
creating outbreaks of violence, generally light,
but with the likelihood of some heavier outbursts,
with conditions remaining reasonably unsettled.
In the west, wildfires continue to dominate
the picture, feeling pleasantly warm, though
with a fairly brisk hurricane moving in from
the coast, there could be a nasty sting in the tail
come teatime. It's all change in the north,
with snow making way for wetter conditions.
Some icy patches remain, but these should clear
from most places by nightfall. Looking further ahead,
there are indications of a front of slow-moving
refugees edging towards the country from all sides,
although there's some uncertainty around this
at present. That's all from me for now.
Do be sure to get out and enjoy that sunshine!

# Skyler and Jeff move in

You worry we'll get too attached if we give them names
but we're not planning on eating them, and anyway

it's too late: since we sided with them over the great tits
scoping the nestbox, they're our bandit-eyed punks,

we've learned their dipping skim and thrum,
their choice of seed and perch.

Jeff's beak was so full of moss he couldn't get in,
you report, although it might have been Skyler,

whom we think is the true workhorse of the pair,
They'll soon be at the feather-lining stage,

I say, having read the RSPB page on nests.
Some people are leaving out funky-coloured wool,

but we agree this is a step too far for Skyler and Jeff,
that we'll observe without intervening,

like that camera crew who filmed the baby elephant
dying of hunger – although I still fret about fledglings

and cats and what we'll really do if the time comes.
Jeff sings from his high branch, Skyler's ready to lay,

we're willing them on. I may take our rainbow down,
after our second jabs, if the chicks survive.

# Late

When Jess pointed out the Tesco car park
where she'd snog married women
on the back seats of their second cars
in the 1990s, reclined on two-kilo bags
of easy cook rice, I knew, as always, I was years
too late, but even so I'd still look for tell-tale steam,
listen for the rustle of multipack crisps
through a chink of wound-down window.
The boys had their cottages and cruising grounds;
I'd never known where to go or how to tell I was there,
astonished, then, to find I must have passed
in the aisles, all this time, all those wives
who'd just popped out to the shops,
and came home hungry, smelling of lentils.

# Everyday heterosexual predicaments: the soap opera

After twenty years the Street is ready for a heterosexual.
Not that it's clear at first. He's just a normal bloke.

Friendly. Doesn't shove it in your face. Decent, even.
Then he starts those over-the-shoulder looks meaning

I'm hugging my boyfriend but really I'm dreaming
of that girl in the corner shop. It's quite sweet,

once you get used to it. Her parents can't know, obviously.
His are dead. A wedding is planned for June. The ratings soar.

No one guesses the ambulance racing to deliver the barmaid's
baby will swerve round a kitten the very second the corner

shop girl steps backwards off the kerb blowing a secret kiss
at his bedroom window. She dies in his arms. He wins a Bafta.

# Colin arrives in Albert Square

Now when we watch TV there's something
making me sit upright, as if I have
a python on my head, and I try to tell if you've

noticed, but there's no way of telling, you're
sitting still too but maybe there's something
else on your mind, maybe every time I have

a python on my head you're worried I have
been ravaged by wolves, and I can't tell if you'd
rather wolves or a python. Either way, there's something.

There's something I have to tell you.

# Haircut, 17

she asks *how much are we taking off today*
and I hear *how much of a lesbian are you*
so I say *oh just half an inch from the top*
but she hasn't finished *do you like it soft
around the ears* she might as well have
asked *how do you like to have sex* and I
don't even know how I like it around
my ears or anywhere else so I just guess
lesbians don't like it soft around their ears
and say *yes yes I do like it soft very soft*
then *shall I use a razor along the back*
oh god will she ever stop *no no razor
thank you* thinking *how can she tell
what has she seen* and she's holding the hand
mirror now to one side then the other
then behind waiting to see what I think
but I've got away with it this time
when I look I'm hardly there at all

# Night run

The thought of it has trailed me all day
like a cooped-up dog, and now my tea's
gone down, I've washed up, watched
the news, I could check my emails again
but know if I give the sofa an inch
it will take a mile – three, actually,
those three I've promised myself
since I didn't go yesterday or the day before,
so it's on with the fluorescent top
and I'm pulling my calf socks up,
thinking I've done the hard bit now,
anything else is a bonus, coaxing my toes
into trainers and out of the front door.
The air's cold enough to gnaw on,
the street so quiet I'm running in velvet
slippers, and it's already worth it,
taking the blind corner a little too fast,
playing roulette with the cyclist
who's never there, endorphins pumping
my arms into superhero fists, feet skipping
the cracks I can't even see. I'm all breath
and blood. Frost prickles my thumbs.
I dart between amber pools, slick as a fish,
know as I leap from the kerb there won't be a car,
not when I'm this invincible, yes, for this
is what I was born for, this bright air,
the whole tingle and spring of it all,
flinging me into the night.

# The hard miles

The first miles, the fast miles,
the lost miles, the last miles,
the cobbly miles, the hobbly miles,
the wobbly after the flu miles,
the dog shit miles, the dog-tired miles,
the dog leg miles, the dead leg miles,
the hungry miles, the hungover miles,
the too-soon-after-tea miles,
the hiccuping miles, the trapped wind miles,
the really-needing-a-wee miles,
the old shoe miles, the new shoe miles,
the stone in the shoe for miles miles,
the itchy miles, the stitchy miles,
the sniffly sodden tissue miles,
the odd sock miles, the wet sock miles,
the sweaty miles, the sweary miles,
the steep miles, the deep heat miles,
the footsteps just behind miles,
the nobody else for miles miles,
the not getting any younger miles,
the not getting any faster miles,
the extra miles, the ultra miles,
the million miles away miles,
the several miles behind miles,
the miles to go before you sleep,
the miles to go before you sleep,
the journey of a thousand miles,
the grit of the single stride.

# Middle-aged     alone     no dog

say it's Thursday in January     fence stubbled with frost
leaves white-furred and crunchy     it might be Monday
in May     or Friday in August     grass luscious or
parched     but you head for the river always     and turn
left     watching gulls strutting on ice     you notice
the man walking towards you     middle-aged     alone
no dog     and start running sums     how fast are his shoes
and yours     which gate is nearest     which key is
sharpest     do rapists wear hats like that     as he closes
and calls     *lovely morning*     your breath is a plume
of guilt in his kindly face     but you still wait
for him to pass     for a gap     wide enough to let go
the phone in your pocket     and when he turns to see
if you've followed     just wide enough to get home

# Missing woman joins search party looking for herself

*Iceland, August 2012*

When I got back from the loo, someone was missing –
about my age, dark hair, black jacket, smaller.

Two people recalled a red hat, but conceded
that might have been somebody else,

perhaps on a previous tour.
The discussion turned to her name

which nobody knew. The bus driver said
we were wasting the light and put us in threes.

I got the couple with matching fleeces and flasks.
It could have been worse: they'd tried,

earlier on, to take me under their wing,
but I've never shared a packed lunch

with anyone, wasn't about to begin,
so we'd stuck to pointing at rocks and nodding.

Now when the wife offered her flask
it felt like starting again, our gloved fingers

glancing, for a moment, around the lid.
I took a good lug. The glow smouldered

all the way back to the canyon.
We spread out, scanning the scrub.

The crags were beautiful now, gilded
with moonlight and rain. Every few minutes,

someone would turn and grin,
raise a thumb or an eyebrow. A team.

And the canyon, so bleak that morning,
rang with yearning for the lost woman,

and for our best selves, the seekers,
calling her in from the dark.

After two hours we stopped for another swig.
I pictured the woman crumpled on a ledge

watching our lights bobbing closer,
the thrill of knowing herself found.

And that was when I realised I was lost.
I let it go on another three hours or so:

searching was so much better for us all,
and how could I explain I wasn't missing,

or rather, that I'd been missing half my life
and I was the last to know?

# Basic life support class

When I re-enter the room,
Susan, you're on the floor,
unresponsive. I lay my cheek
to your mouth, watch your ribs
not rising, shout for help,
place the heel of my hand
on your chest, pump, count,
think of you, Susan, kneeling
with me by Resusci-Anne,
calling her name, tilting her chin,
closing our lips around hers.

I want a badge for my swimsuit,
Susan, to be best friends again,
but you have the face of a girl
who drowned in the Seine
and my mouth tastes of rubber.
Your breasts are beige,
unblemished. Can you hear me,
Susan? How many breaths
should it take to bring you back?
How will I know when to stop?

# Pomander

blunt
hedgehog
shrunken   planet
nail-studded light bulb
canker-riddled armadillo
red-ribboned ague charm
rotten-bellied      bauble
clove-poxed grenade
winter's   heart
cured

# Dark Peak, February

stone walls lean green-furred
faces into horizontal hail

snowdrops nod huddled heads
at mute daffodil spears

starlings witter and wheel
tumbling to earth like leaves

water gnaws the track's edge
where the chaffinch hops

under lightning-black twigs
catkins dance like drying socks

# Pandemic recovery plan

When it comes, let me crawl under the patchwork quilt
of a late Edwardian novel, with a ginger cat
curled at the foot of my bed, and a coal fire
flicking in a light breeze from the casement.

Four siblings take it in turns to play charades;
a fifth, with a weak chest, sends up sherbet lemons;
and a forbidden friend on the lawn blinks
*Get well soon* with a hurricane lamp.

A housekeeper brings broth and chamomile tea
on a tray with a vase of primroses,
and a kindly doctor bearing a Gladstone bag
ushers a vigil until my fever breaks.

After three nights of cold flannels and prayers,
a thrush trills on the windowsill and I wake,
apple-cheeked, asking how long I have slept.
I am teaspooned with tonic and wheeled into the sun.

It is almost summer, but I won't remember
the year, or how to find the way back,
which will be overgrown with thorns in any case
and all the breadcrumbs gone.

# What they didn't teach us on the PGCE

Which questions to answer. What to do
with a dropped tissue. How to stand back.
How to hold your breath. What not to hand out.
When to hide in the loo. How to go to school
the day the newsreader's voice cracks.
How to give out books without touching them.
When to turn away. How to wash your hands
after the soap runs out. How to stay at home.
How to sit at a desk. How to listen to a missing
homework. When to switch off. How silent
a Chat can be. What to say to the dad who doesn't
want any of that school bollocks in his house.
How to go back. What to leave behind. How
to teach poems in a lab. How to command
respect in a mask. What to forget. How to fill holes.
What that cough doesn't mean. When to breathe.
How to spot confusion from two metres.
What not to take in. How many bananas you need.
What to say to the boy whose mum died
after he brought it home. How much
you can carry. Why there is never enough tea.

# Chalk

You brought it home like contraband
in orange packs that bore our name,
*Binney & Smith*, so my fingers and thumb
held it snug early on, as I practised being you
for my class of bunnies and mice.
It mingled with smoke on your blouse,
the staffroom fug that lodged in your lung
and killed you before we had time
to mark what was yours, what was mine,
what lay between and behind. Your tin
now rests on my desk, with its sleek
blues and reds, the stub-ends of yellow
and white, just our fingertips' size.

# Weight

We had a way
of cooking
together
that I know
only by its
absence
in other
women.

If I were
peeling
potatoes,
say,
and you
needed to fill
the kettle,
you'd reach
round and I'd
lean a little
to the left
to let you
at the tap.

You'd dart
from cooker
to fridge
the way
that startles
others
when I
do it now,
but I'd always
know where
you were.

This, then,
is grief,
or at least
mine: less
the absence
of you,
more the
weight
of myself
with others
where once
we were
light.

# Spice rack

They jostled like kids in a class photo –
moody cardamom, bossy cloves, peculiar fenugreek,
stubborn ginger, cosy nutmeg, spiky paprika –

the homely ones – cinnamon, fennel, mace –
and the glamorous ones – turmeric, garam masala,
star anise – watching through trim wooden rails

as your fingers found mine in the dough,
pressing squeals from my fingers,
while the saucepans chattered on the hob.

In the corner of my kitchen, dusty-shouldered,
by your wooden spoons, they murmur of casserole
and crumble, mulled wine and saffron buns.

# Come to the cookhouse door

Your tales were like *Judy, Patrol Leader*,
which I read between Brownies and Guides:
the too-curious cows, the campfires, the storms,
the jelly baby that turned out to be a slug.
The proof was your blanket and badges,
the sheath-knife in your underwear drawer,
your whittling of marshmallow skewers.

I tie a clove hitch your way, still, hands
crossed, one loop passed behind the other.
Your whistle swings from my lanyard. Sometimes
at break, in the frenzy of footballs and bags,
I blow for the Captains and Judys, and for their
stalwart Seconds, for all the Swallows, Blackbirds
and Robins, for the Bluebells and Thistles, for you.

# When you give a plant to a teacher

We will thank you very much and say
how lovely it will look on our desk.
We will mean it, then pop it on the fridge.
It will be watered once a week, at first,
then maybe once a month, once a term.
It will turn so brown and limp an English teacher
will use it as a prompt. For thirty teenagers,
for an hour, it will become a symbol of hope,
desiccated. Three students will write their best
poem that day. Twenty-seven will think
*it's just a fucking plant get over it.*
Back in the staffroom, it will yield a limb
to soothe a sunburned PE teacher. An Art trainee
will name it Vera, until a Science technician
will say it should be Alan, actually.
The PE teacher will regret rubbing Alan
on her legs. Alan will outgrow his pot
and be taken home like the class rabbit.
When he returns in a tub, the Head of Drama
will suggest *Little Shop of Horrors*
for the school show. But there will be larvae
in his new compost, and soon break
is bedevilled with flies. Suspicion
must fall upon Alan. He will be banished
to the garden of the pupil referral unit.
No one comes back from there.
He will languish beside beans, gone over,
two gnomes and a plastic hedgehog.
Even then, he will be fine, until the first frost
transfigures his leaves into swords.
He will be borne inside and thawed
with the surplus water from a Pot Noodle.
The next day, he will resemble a squashed
octopus. There will seem no hope for Alan.
But a teaching assistant will coax a boy
to chop Alan back to his roots with safety
scissors. It's better than Maths anyway,

and as he hacks and swears, he will care
to tip the putrid sap back on the soil,
mumbling about nutrients and shit. And
two months will pass, and no one will think
about Alan, until the teaching assistant spots
lime-green shoots nudging the stump
and sends a photo: *Is it wrong that it made me
a bit emotional???* When you give a plant
to a teacher, you may think we like to tend,
but we tend haphazardly. What we will
do is notice; what we'll do well is share.

# Ditton Meadow

It's never the same, whatever *it* is,
after a walk on the meadow,
the chonk of the gate
always an opening out
and a bringing back.
Today, a crust of frost
unlocking bog
impassable for weeks.
Yesterday, terns skimming the river,
six cormorants in a tree.
Often, cattle – the whole herd
blocking the gap,
or a lone calf,
having shimmied over the grid,
standing on the bridge,
chewing.
Once, you brought me a barn owl
ghosting the reeds,
and I brought you a heron
lancing a fish.
That year the river froze,
together we brought back
the whump of our torch on the ice.
And one spring dawn,
the day she died,
we learned to untangle
one song from another,
bringing home robin and blackbird,
blackcap and wren,
the marsh tit's squeaky *atchoo*.
Sometimes, in bed, we'll say
*Remember that time when*

and it might be the cow
stuck in the hedge
that looked like a plastic bag,
or the woman who'd stepped
on a swarm of bees.

When we're ninety, you'll still be saying
*Remember when those dogs chased us*
*and we legged it over the fence?*
And I will. I reckon I will.

# Desire lines

each set of   locked-down feet
reaching   the same tussock
or root made   the same choice
to skirt right or left   to step
two metres   off the paved path
to make   space

we didn't see   the others
only spotting   weeks later
we'd sketched   the same invisible
ink curves   all over meadow
and park   each solitary
rationed walk   tracing
a shared   desire
amid thistle   and mud

# Straight-line mission

woolly willow   nc *because they* ptarmigan   hooded crow   scottish wildcat
mountain hare   sc *were the first because* en hoverfly   red squirrel   shining guest ant
pine marten   fres *of the simplicity of it* 
crested tit   wood ant *because they had tired* aver capercaillie   curlew   oblong woodsia
*of hikes across Alpine* they
beauty   pine hoverfly *ridges because* they ng   kentish glory   waxcaps   dark bordered
*because it was a great*
aspen twinflower   o *thought it was they were* february red stonefly   northern damselfly
*idea because watching*
sow thistle   small cow i *inspired by* snow bunting   marsh saxifrage   alpine blue
fly   ptarmigan   hoode *straight-line mission* n bee   woolly willow   northern silver stiletto
*because they*
aspen hoverfly   red sq *videos because of* mountain hare   scabious mining bee
*were in search*
beaver capercaillie   cu *genuine novelty* t   pine marten   freshwater pearl mussel
*of 988,000*
waxwing   kentish gl *because subscribers* crested tit   wood ant   golden eagle
*YouTube were*
northern february red stor *because they* rdered beauty   pine hoverfly   snow flea
*explorers in a*
wintergreen   snow bunting *budding where every* y   aspen   twinflower   one-flowered
*world is mapped*
pinewood mason bee   wooll *corner* e blue sow thistle   small cow wheat
scottish wildcat   mountain h *because of the beautiful* r stiletto fly   ptarmigan   hooded crow
*countryside*
shining guest ant   pine marten *Scottish they used* e   aspen hoverfly   red squirrel
oblong woodsia   crested tit   t *because poles to wade* l   beaver capercaillie   curlew
*walking waist-high*
dark bordered beauty   pine ho *through because they* waxwing   kentish glory   waxcaps
*heather because they*
damselfly aspen twinflower *enjoyed about half of* hern february red stonefly   northern
*it was*
saxifrage alpine blue sow thistle *it because* een   snow bunting   marsh
*because because*
northern silver stiletto fly   ptarmiga *it addictive* ewood mason bee   woolly willow
*was not the most fun*
scabious mining bee   aspen hoverfly *route because the* sh wildcat   mountain hare
*the guest ant   pine marten*
freshwater pearl mussel   beaver *challenge of sticking to* oblong woodsia   crested tit
*the straight line was so*
wood ant   golden eagle   waxwing *because* dark bordered beauty   pine
*compelling made it*
hoverfly snow flea   northern february *technology the* damselfly   aspen
*easier because of the*
twinflower   one-flowered wintergreen *concentration* h saxifrage   alpine blue sow
thistle   small cow wheat   pinewo *utter because of illow* northern silver
*because it was one of*
stiletto fly   ptarmigan   hooded crow *the few experiences* ain hare   scabious mining
*of genuine adventure*
bee   aspen hoverfly   red squirrel *because they marten wintergreen* snow
*available because they heat* pinewood mason
bunting   marsh saxifrage   alpine blu *asked for advice the* hooded crow   scottish
bee   woolly willow   northern silv *were on how to repeat the* squirrel   shining guest
wildcat   mountain hare   scabious mining be *journey because they* e blue sow thistle
ant   pine marten wintergreen   snow bunting *were too exhausted to*
small cow wheat   pinewood mason bee   wo *were truly celebrate because* lver stiletto fly   mining bee   aspen
ptarmigan   hooded crow   scottish wildcat n *these things get in*
*your head*

# On stagnant deeps

*after Elizabeth Willis, after Erasmus Darwin*

Stick a rat's tail in your pocket. Stay at home. Old Johnny Axey, Bailiff of the Marshes, creeps through sedge-wove bog on webbed feet. Beware the quakes. Pull your sleeve over your palm to shut the gate. Don't touch your face. Watch where Lord John Fever shakes his clotted hair. 'Tis a horrid air for a stranger to breathe in. Keep your distance. Build your house on stilts above the fog. Wash your hands. Stay alert. Rub rabbit droppings in oil, coat with flour, fry. Save lives. Dose the babes with poppy-head tea. Go to work. There's plenty more brides in the uplands. Next slide please.

# Heeling in at Lower Wood

We work in pairs: one digging and planting,
the other setting guards and hammering stakes,
swapping every few trees to switch muscles,
the clay so thick we jump on the spade
then rock, front to back, side to side
to prise it out. Checking the size of each cleft,
we pick from bundles in sacks: oak for a deep one,
willow for a skinny one, hazel for a wide one,
tucking the roots down and heeling them in.

Two weeks from the end of the second year,
the day after my third jab, every damn sapling
is a metaphor, or an omen, and it can't
just be me thinking, this is the way
to spend an apocalypse: planting a wood,
pressing the earth snug, the warden nodding,
saying, *That's good heeling in, that is.*

# On Wonder Woman's Island

the women are all leather and deltoids,
sword fights and whirling hair. They
call *You are stronger than you know,*
reaching out sinewy forearms to lift
each other up off the sand. Any time
you can yell *Shield!* just for the hell of it
and a girl will kneel, shield angled over thigh,
while another runs up, springs, fires an arrow
mid-leap, lands on a silver horse. At night
there's a cave with an underground
waterfall jacuzzi and a nook in the wall
thick with fur. And if the men come,
lugging guns up the beach, you sleep on,
cat-like: seeing only sheer cliffs and bare rock
they will soon turn tail, their flag not worth
the planting here, and the breeze long gone.

# Courtship

Football fizzled out, but you emailed to say
you missed running round chasing a ball –
would I like to play tennis? I'm useless at tennis,

but missed running round chasing balls,
or rather, chasing the same ball as you,
which was what I hoped you meant.

We set a date. It rained. And again, the next week.
I wondered if someone who enjoyed
chasing balls might also fancy a drink.

You called, inviting me for a drink.
We chatted about ex-boyfriends, the Indigo Girls,
wearing suits to family weddings. The list

of things you liked grew longer, more hopeful.
We made another date, vowing to play
come rain or shine. The sun shone

on our first set, and I chased missed balls,
until fat drops spattered the court, and we ran
for the brick shelter where we'd first met.

A month later, in bed, you said it was my arms
that did it – the way I'd hugged myself warm
just where you wanted to stroke, and I revealed

I'd wished my hands were yours.
The thing is, nothing happened that day,
in the shelter, in the summer storm,

but that was the last time we ever stood, no net
between us, wanting and not touching,
and it was enough, lovely E, it was enough.

# How we knew

I think when you told me you'd chosen the wine
because you liked the picture on the bottle,
while I was setting the oven gloves on fire
and trying to pretend I hadn't. And when
you admitted you'd flirted from your end
of the tennis court the whole summer,
and I confessed I was too short-sighted to see.
The individual chocolate mousses clinched it.

Then you knew and I knew and the evening
stretched before us, the air fat with so much
knowing it hurt to breathe, and I didn't know
what to do, and neither did you, until, somehow,
we did: hands, lips, skin, my single bed
rocking with laughter, long after dark.

# Opening

Every Christmas I wonder what my aunt is thinking
sending us separate cards, in separate envelopes,
with separate stamps, to the same address.

Perhaps the allure of the burly postman,
sweating under the double weight of mail,
will turn my gaze, at last, from your smile.

Perhaps the extra reaching down, picking up,
opening, reading, means today
I will leave for work without a kiss.

Perhaps we will fight over whose card
takes pride of place, fall out, fall silent,
fall into separate beds, separate. Yes, they know

what they are doing, these separate-card senders,
and therefore so must we, sharing cards, homes,
wounds, opening ourselves out.

# Exposure

*'My party has done a huge amount to support LGBT rights... But at the same time I also agree that it's right that parents should be able to choose the moment at which their children become exposed to that information.'*

*Andrea Leadsom MP, March 2019*

Dear Parent/Carer

If you have not yet chosen the moment
to expose your child to the information

of our existence, please indicate this by ticking
the appropriate box at the bottom of this poem.

We will then take the necessary steps to ensure
no further contact with your child.

Should accidental exposure occur, such as
the formation of friendships with our offspring,

being in close proximity to public handholding
(or similar) your child may exhibit the following

symptoms: curiosity, empathy, loss of prejudice.
These effects are usually temporary, if normal

conditions are quickly restored. Report the incident
to the relevant authorities, who will activate

further protective measures for your child
until the run-up to his/her sixteenth birthday,

at which point we will resume teaching, guarding,
entertaining, serving and nursing him/her.

# When we hold hands

*after Richard Scott*

they don't always
know how to go

my right turned in
your left turned out

or the other way round
twisting one way then

the other like teenagers
so used after so long

to how we fit in
the dark it's strange

this not-knowing how
we fit in the street

where our held hands
hold a middle finger

up where we are still
dangerous dykes

# Like a fish

It's never a woman
unicycling down the road,

always a lone man
wiggling his hips atop

a brakeless wheel, no
basket, lights, helmet,

nothing holding him up
save that dogged halibut

stare into middle
age. Just one look

and you know why a fish
needs this even less.

# Everyday heterosexual predicaments:
## the mini-break

The heterosexual couple arrive at the B & B
feeling a little on edge. Will their booking

have disappeared? Will they be asked
if they are siblings, cousins or friends?

They are shown to the double en suite with
an apology – the twin room's already taken,

if only the owner had known he'd have swapped
things round – but they must give their assent

to this arrangement with just the right shade
of approval, minus the enthusiasm

which might declare an intention to have sex,
a thought which hovers over the duvet

nonetheless, the landlord wondering what it is
straight people do anyway and whether this bed

is up to it, the heterosexuals watching him
wondering, longing for Scrabble and tea.

# Tea & coffee at 8.25

*from Anne Lister's final diary entry, 11th August 1840.*

I picture the other Ann in the wicker barn
shaking out blankets on straw,
unwrapping cups, measuring coffee and tea.

Outside, settling horses and men,
Anne notes wooded hills rising
to conical summits over their heads,

calculates distance and time. Ann pours.
Anne strides in, holds their cheese
to the lamp, scanning for cat-hair.

I picture an evening, then, so like the rest
there is nothing to say. I picture
an evening like this one, ours,

stroking your face on my lap between
bath and bed, and all those pages ahead.

# Sleeping together

I climb into bed, you say,
like a young bullock,

quite the feat
for a small woman,

though perhaps outdone,
I say, by your trick

of rolling yourself
into a duvet roulade.

Twenty-two years
of lying together here,

my breaths no longer
vexing your deaf ear,

yours a steady swash
on my fears' shore.

# Grain

some nights      after we close our books
you crawl under my arm      and tell me

how we were carved from the same tree
the top of your head      from my chin

my hand      from your ribs      the same grain
running through both of us all the way

from my ear to your little toe and back up
so      rolling towards sleep      moored

to your deepening breath      I count
all our rings      from heartwood to bark

# Pitch drop experiment

In 1927 Professor Thomas Parnell poured hot tar into a funnel, let it settle for
three years, then cut the stem so that the pitch formed a drop which swelled
like a balloon before falling for the first time in 1938, then again roughly
once every decade, thereby proving the viscosity of bitumen to be
about 230 billion times greater than that of water, in the world's
longest continuously-running experiment, which I view on the
livestream from the University of Queensland, the next blob
poised, a slick black bulb, like the bottle of Baby Bio Dad
wielded every Sunday watering the houseplants after
church, so that now, watching the webcam,
a new experiment begins, words poured
through the neck of a poem
slowing    to
the speed
of tar
as I
see
my
father
counting
drops into
the pale blue
indoor   watering
can,  tending   orchids,
steady-handed,  the whole
house smelling of roast
beef  and  Yorkshires,
four  drops  of
bitumen
ago

# Christmas Eve in Dad's kitchen

and now only I know which bits of Delia
we follow, which we skip, and what

*The Dairy Book of Home Cookery (1968)*
still knows best. I know to find the stump-handled

jug for the cranberry jelly, and why eight pints
of milk is probably just enough, factoring in

bread sauce and white sauce and people
wanting extra cups of tea because so much

rich food is bound to make them thirsty.
I know how to arrange the little cottage

on the cake beside the bald tree, and Santa
listing up the piped path, know even to dib

two sets of hoof-prints behind his reindeer.
I know when to fetch the turkey from the garage

to warm up, and what she would have done
with the giblets, which I won't.

When everyone's asleep, only I know
I open the jar of cloves she sealed last year

and breathe her in.

# Distance

the carrots my brother buys are the wrong ones
Dad tells me so he had to go to the supermarket
we've told him not to go to where he waited
half an hour outside chatting to a lovely girl
he doesn't know what all the fuss is about loo roll
I'm trying to find new ways to say you can walk
to the shops and back just don't go inside
is it worth risking your life for carrots I think
of the shopping basket handle how long he takes
to choose the people reaching round breathing
the queue for the till the couple he will have
befriended in front I ask if he washes
his hands as soon as he gets home but he wants
to tell me about the robins' nest above the back door
so I tell him about the moorhen chicks
and for the rest of the call we offer up birds
into the sixty miles thirty years between us
his saying let me go mine saying Dad don't die

# Guinea pig

My brother calls to tell me the Police
have picked up our Dad, walking back

from the opticians along the motorway,
and I think of that term we waited ten weeks

for our turn to bring Ginger Susie home;
how she slunk through my brother's hands

the first morning, and slipped under the neighbours' hedge.
We weigh up whether to return Dad's car key now

or to wait until his glasses have been fixed.
*He has twelve boxes of cup-a-soup in the cupboard*

I say, and we try to work out if that's good
or bad. It's one or the other. My brother

will sort the dentist, I'll sort the chiropodist.
Neither of us mentions the roof.

Somewhere, we are still six and eight,
kneeling by a hedge in the dusk, holding out carrots.

# I cut, you choose

The day you became my brother,
Dad slipped an ambulance
into my cot, a gift for you, too small
to smell a bribe, who learned
that this was what sisters did:
they knew what you'd always wanted,
and took what you'd always had.

You can't recall life before
your six and my half dozen,
your yellow, my red, your soldiers,
my farm. You nicked a Yorkie
and I kept watch. I cut, you chose.
We hit as hard as we liked
as long as it didn't bruise.

If we met as strangers now,
we'd have nothing to say.
Still, when the phone rings
and it's you, and it's Dad again,
I'm glad of the hours of *Guess Who?*
the pick 'n' mix, the going round
together to ask for our football back.

# Sunday lunch

I bring our lunch in my pack.
Through the jasmine-fringed window
you look up from the kitchen sink,
searching for something lost.

Through the jasmine-fringed window
I read you for a moment, unseen,
searching for something lost.
You wave and open the door.

For a moment I read you, unseen:
coming home to my father, I find a child.
You wave and open the door,
rummaging for my name.

Coming home to my father, I see a child
look up from the kitchen sink
and rummage for the woman's name
who brings his lunch in her pack.

# The women of 10y3

Getting you out of hospital is the latest thing
I think I should know how to do, and don't,
but I have Donna's number on a post-it.
I'm not sure who Donna is but when she picks up
and calls me *darling* I nearly cry.
You're not her remit any more, Donna says,
but she hands me over to Hollie
who calls Amber from Respite Care.
Hollie will get you transferred this afternoon
and once you're settled, Keeley and Kayleigh
will be in touch. And now we have a plan,
and I know it will be OK because we both
trust these women with the names of girls
who sat at the backs of our classrooms years ago,
you about to retire, me just starting out,
the ones who'd warn us when a lad farted,
who cared enough to chew without us seeing,
the ones who'd lend a highlighter, and print
coursework in 14 pt with bordered hearts.
Sometimes they'd be off and we'd find out
there was a brother with Down's or a nan
who wanted the company, and it would make sense,
then, that point they'd made about Juliet and the Nurse,
when we'd picked on them one Friday afternoon,
and realised there was more going on.
They're tattooed now, often, which you enjoy.
It's something to chat over while they're helping
you on with your socks, the hearts filled
with children's names, the no-good men
morphed into dolphins. They make it all look
as easy as you once made poems seem, or tried to,
these impressive capable Ambers and Dawns
who've learned to read between your lines,
to breathe warmth into a hard word.
And now Hollie with the mermaid tattoo,
coming down the ward with her clipboard,
who will sign your discharge papers
with a circle over the i, then follow me out
to ask if you'd like a man to change your pad.

# The speed of spring

Today I heard that spring moves across the UK
at 1.9 miles per hour

and I thought of the bluebells
I brought to the ward

a week after our last lunch
in your own garden.

The cow parsley's in flower now
and you're back inside.

I bring you hares in a buttercup field
from the train window.

You look out at the car park
seeking the word *swift*.

Something untold is moving within you
faster than hawthorn.

# Quinquireme

The man in the next bed
    ponders when bin day might fall
    after the long weekend.

I watch his wife reach in her bag,
      then withdraw her hand,
    phoneless,
opting, rather,
    for this mulling,
the language of home
      that holds and hides them
  a while
      longer.

That was your language,
                once,
    but now
  your words
        are marvellous,
                  rare.

I read the poems
  we have by heart
  and you whisper with me

  *runcible*

    *quinquireme*

    *casement*

      *Innisfree*

# Shed

Dad, when I say your mind is like a garden shed,
think of ours, forest green, the shed you came to fix
that summer after our bikes got nicked. And when I say
think of our garden shed, I know you can't, anymore,
so here's that photo of you leaning against it,
with your drill and the burglar-proof bar you fitted,
which, by the way, still holds. And when you see that photo,
think of our bikes inside, the ones that replaced the ones
that got nicked, chained with the hardened steel shackle
you bolted to the floor. And when you remember those bolts,
think how we joked about the poor future thief,
hacking through the burglar-proof bar, only to find our bikes
shackled up with hardened steel. And when I ask you to think
of the bikes and the hard steel shackle and the burglar-proof bar
and the bolts and the summer's day and the drill,
I'm trying to say that I catch you listening to yourself,
some days, Dad, like that thief locked out of our shed.

# Notes

*The opposite of Swedish death cleaning:* 'Döstädning' is known in English as 'Swedish death cleaning' – a method of decluttering one's house, often in late middle age, in preparation for death.

*Muscle memory:* The copper font in Norwich Cathedral was gifted in 1994 by the Rowntree Mackintosh chocolate factory, having previously been used to make toffee.

*Sestina for a lost boi:* 'Boi' is slang for a young, gender-nonconforming lesbian.

*Testimony:* This poem was sourced from a social media forum where people shared experiences of other Christians' responses to their coming out as lesbian or gay.

*The mysterious starling:* The bird referenced in this poem, *aplonis mavornata*, is known by only one specimen, which was shot 'hopping about [on a] tree' by its discoverer, Andrew Bloxam, naturalist of HMS Blonde, in 1825. The species is now extinct. The parts of this poem in italics are taken from the Wikipedia entry for the 'Mauke Starling', or 'mysterious starling'.

*How to conquer nature:* The title of this poem was influenced by the slogan of Chairman Mao's Four Pests Campaign: 'Man must conquer nature'. Part of the Great Leap Forward, Mao's War on Sparrows began in 1958 and is now deemed to have been a significant factor in causing the Great Famine, which killed an unknown number of Chinese citizens, thought to be in excess of 45 million.

*Missing woman joins search party looking for herself:* This title was inspired by a headline which appeared in multiple news outlets in August 2012.

*Straight-line mission:* On 30th September 2021 a pair of hikers became the first people to walk the longest straight line in the UK without crossing a paved road, after spending four days crossing 78.55km (48.8 miles) from the Pass of Drumochter to Corgarff in north Scotland. Their route passed through the Cairngorms National Park, which is home to 25% of the UK's most endangered species.

*On stagnant deeps:* This poem is inspired by Elizabeth Willis's collection *Meteoric Flowers*, a meditation on Erasmus Darwin's famous work *The Botanic Garden*. The title *On stagnant deeps*, and other phrases within the poem, are taken from Darwin's description of the Fens. Other phrases from the poem are borrowed from folk cures for the fen ague, sourced from *The Fenland Ague in the Nineteenth Century* by Alice Nicholls, as well as from public information campaign material circulated during the first year of the Covid-19 pandemic.

*Tea & coffee at 8.25:* The title of this poem is the final sentence in Anne Lister's diary, written on the evening of 11th August 1840, while Anne was traveling through Georgia with her partner Ann Walker. This last diary entry begins with Anne having been woken between 1 and 2 in the morning by 'cats at my cheese.' She died of a fever on 22nd September 1840.

# Acknowledgements

Acknowledgements are due to the editors of the following publications in which some of these poems first appeared: *The Bridport Prize Anthology 2019; Butcher's Dog; The Fenland Poetry Journal; Ink, Sweat and Tears; The North; Under the Radar; The Rialto; Poetry Village; The Interpreter's House; Renard Press; Poetry for Good; Live Canon Anthology 2022; The Passionfruit Review; Spelt; Magma; Ginkgo Prize Anthology 2022; South Downs Poetry Festival Anthology 2023; Frogmore Press; Strix; The Result is What you See Today; Mslexia; Poetry Birmingham Literary Journal.*

Although my parents are unable to read these poems, I felt their presences so strongly whilst sorting and clearing their house, as well as while writing some of the poems in this collection. A particular joy was finding their tins of chalk (both of which appear on this book cover), and feeling a jolt of connection, as if they were passing on tiny batons, one teacher to another. I have worked hard to claim a space for writing in the midst of a busy teaching career; finding my parents' chalk felt as if it brought the different parts of my life together, and I am grateful for that connection between us, as well as for all the other points of connection that keep them present in my life despite death and dementia.

It's a particular honour to receive an endorsement for this collection from Barbara Bleiman, who is such a voice of wisdom and sanity for English teachers, as well as being a fine fellow poet. Thank you to all my teacher friends, and in particular to Helen Parfect, Sean Dooley, Caroline Powell, Kate Barker, Emma Hayward, Lizzi Rawlinson-Mills and Gabrielle Cliff Hodges. Between you, you keep my faith in the best sort of English teaching at a time when it's sorely needed. And thank you for saying, 'You should write a poem about that' only slightly more often than is tolerable; I hope you enjoy spotting the poems that resulted from your suggestions.

Several poems in this collection began their lives on Poetry School courses tutored by Catherine Smith, and I am hugely grateful to Catherine for setting such carefully-considered writing tasks, for providing such detailed and generous feedback, and for managing the fortnightly online chats in such a supportive way. Those live chats were some of my most open-hearted online experiences during the Covid-19 pandemic.

First audiences matter for all poets, and especially for relatively late starters like me. The warmth of Fen Speak, skilfully hosted by Beth Hartley and

Stewart Carswell, welcomed several of these poems into the world for the first time. Holly Henderson continues to be the best first reader I could wish for, and a steady, heartening presence in my corner. And I am so grateful to have been adopted by the wonderful Cambridge U3A Twenty-First Century Poets group, who discuss my poems in front of me with a much shrewder understanding than I have, and then take me out for lunch.

I am particularly grateful to Jo Clement of *Butcher's Dog* for championing my poetry at an early stage, when her backing played a significant role in building my confidence. I will be forever indebted to the *Mslexia* Poetry Pamphlet Competition for opening such a significant door for me in getting *Other Women's Kitchens* published. And Rebecca Goss has been a fearlessly honest, supportive and challenging poetry mentor at several points over the last few years. Thank you for taking me seriously when I only had a handful of poems, and for helping me to see the wood for the trees when it came to assembling this collection.

Once again I am so fortunate to have been able to call upon the huge talent, patience and creative vision of Kate Winter for the cover art. Thank you so much for the gift of capturing so many precious artefacts in such a bold and ingenious way.

And thank you to the whole team at Seren Books, and especially to poetry editors Zoë Brigley and Rhian Edwards, for all your hard work in bringing this collection together. Your insights into the sequencing of the poems were pivotal.

To Nicola Norbury, thank you for always being there for me, and particularly for being with me that day in the house, and for completely understanding why we needed to bring back forty set squares, a boot-load of sewing materials and a piano accordion.

Finally, deepest thanks to my partner in life, Emily McMullen, who is just as brilliant at giving feedback on early drafts as she is at clearing a house, who was patient with many of the random items I wanted to keep, and who also knew when and how to draw the line.